WILF the MIGHTY WORRIER

SAVES THE WORLD

For my boys

First published in Great Britain in 2015 by
Quercus Publishing Ltd
This edition published in 2016 by
Hodder and Stoughton

ISBN 978 1 84866 8 614

The paper and board used in this book
are made from wood from responsible sources

MIX
Paper from
responsible sources
FSC® C104740

10 9 8 7

Printed and bound in Great Britain by Clays Ltd, St Ives plc

Quercus Children's Books
An imprint of
Hachette Children's Group
Part of Hodder and Stoughton
Carmelite House
50 Victoria Embankment
London EC4Y 0DZ

WILF THE MIGHTY WORRIER

SAVES THE WORLD

Georgia Pritchett

CHAPTER 1
THE BEGINNING

Hey, you! Yes, you. Come over here a minute.

Come closer.

Come CLOSER.

Come CLOSER...

Not that CLOSE!

1

OK. Now listen. I've got something to tell you. It's very important.

And it's a **secret**.

Just between me and you and no one else. Promise you won't tell anyone? Good.

Right, well, you know the world? Yes. *The world*. That great big round thing you're standing on. Well, that nearly ended. Yes it did. Last week. And not in a good way.

Oh, there was a great

BIG KERFUFFLE

and I know exactly what happened – and I don't mind telling *you*, but I don't want anyone else to know. OK? So, you know that boy called WILF? Yes you do. Yes you dooooooooo! That small tiny one from school. His hair's sort of scruffly like this. And his ears are kind of pingy like this. And his head's so full of ideas it's like busy bees packing for their holiday inside his brain.

Remember now? Yes! Him! Well, he saved the world. He did. Honestly.

Now, WILF isn't your typical superhero. For a start, he doesn't have a cape. Plus, he can't fly. Or climb tall buildings. Which is probably a good thing because he's scared of heights. In fact, he's scared of quite a lot of things – so many things that he has made a list so that he can remember them. This is his list:

WILF'S
LIST OF THINGS
I AM OFFICIALLY SCARED OF

Stuffed animals
Creepy-crawlies with zillions of legs
Creepy-crawlies that have
Waggly feeler things instead of eyes
Sea monsters

Peanut butter getting stuck to the
  roof of my mouth
Wigs
Roller skates
Moths
Lifts
Dogs pushing me out of the
  window while I'm asleep
Twirly moustaches
Polo-neck jumpers
Loud noises
Vikings

Admittedly, you don't see many Vikings
these days but that doesn't stop Wilf worrying
that he *might* see a Viking. You see, Wilf is
a bit of a worrier. He worries all the time. If
worrying was an Olympic sport, he would be

5

worrying whether he was going to get picked for the team. And it would probably be best if he *wasn't* picked for the team because he's allergic to Lycra. Come to think of it, Wilf is allergic to loads of things:

Wheat
Dairy
His own dandruff
Flowers (make me wheeze)
Cows (make me sneeze)
Horses (make my eyes go red)
Damp (makes me cough)
Spicy food (makes me hiccup)

Sometimes it isn't easy being Wilf. But he is *good* at a lot of things too, like:

6

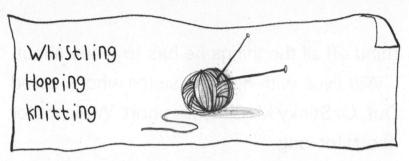

Whistling
Hopping
knitting

All right, that's only three things he's good at – but he's *really* good at those three things.

He can do puffy-out whistles, sucky-in whistles and a whistle that sounds a bit like a grasshopper playing a tiny flute.

He can also hop. Hopping is lucky. He can do long hops and high hops and big skippety hops. And he's very good at knitting, which is useful for taking his

mind off all the things he has to worry about.

Wilf lives with his little sister who is called Dot. Or Stinky McGinty for short. Well, not for short, for long.

Dot has a crusty face and is generally a bit sticky. Her main interests are eating things and hammering. In her spare time she makes smells. Because she's a baby and that's what babies do.

Dot has a favourite teddy that is actually a pig called Pig. Pig used to be pink and fluffy but now he is grey and shiny and smells like an old mop. That's just what happens when you love things a lot and don't wash them very often.

Wilf's best friend is his pet woodlouse called Stuart. They've been together since back in the olden days when Wilf was only five. Wilf and Stuart are soulmates. They understand each other's funny little ways. They like all the same things. They finish each other's sentences. Actually, that's not true because Stuart can't talk, but Wilf doesn't say much either so, in a way, they finish each other's silences.

Stuart looks up to Wilf. He wishes he could have ideas like Wilf does. He wishes he could whistle like Wilf does. He even wishes he could *knit* like Wilf does – but he can't do any of those things because he is tiny and he has a tiny brain and no lips and no thumbs.

Wilf loves Stuart.

Sometimes he wishes he *was* Stuart because then he could scrunch up in a ball and roll away when things get difficult. But that isn't allowed when you're a human. He tried it once at a birthday party and people had looked at him strangely.

Wilf also lives with his mum who is a grown-up but she can't help it and Wilf tries to make allowances. Mum has a job which is very complicated and involves a lot of making phone calls and being nice to people and a lot of saying rude words when she hangs up.

Anyway – where was I? Oh yes, the world ending. So it nearly did – and it was a *little bit very scary*, I can tell you. Take my word for it.

What?

What? You're not going to take my word for it? I have to tell you what happened? But I'm busy!

Sheesh! All right, stop your badgering and listen carefully. I'll start from the very beginning . . .

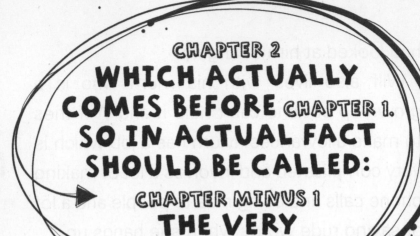

CHAPTER 2
WHICH ACTUALLY COMES BEFORE CHAPTER 1. SO IN ACTUAL FACT SHOULD BE CALLED:
CHAPTER MINUS 1
THE VERY BEGINNING

Once upon a time, great big tall high dinosaurs roamed the earth.

Then one day one of them said, 'Let's have a massive game of hide-and-seek!'

So all the dinosaurs hid, but they forgot to pick anyone to do the seeking, so they're not actually extinct,

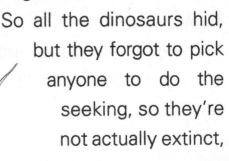

they're just hiding. It's true! Ask *anyone* if you don't believe me.

So then not much happened for about a kerbillion years and then I think it got a bit parky and then—

Hang on, I think I've started this story *too* far back. Let's go forward a bit.

Once upon a time, an alien said, 'Gleep. Piddleydoo piddleydoo plip plim xlank.'

Oh no! Now I've gone too far forward!

OK. How about if we start when somebody moved into the house next door to Wilf. A big removal lorry arrived outside and Wilf rushed upstairs to peep through the window on the landing. He wondered whether it might be a boy with really great toys. Or maybe a girl with really great toys. Or maybe a kindly old lady who liked to spend her days giving sweets to the boy next door.

But when Wilf saw his new neighbour he was very disappointed. It wasn't a girl and it wasn't a boy and it wasn't a kindly old lady. It was a small man. The small-man-next-door had a lot of stuff. Because the small-man-next-door was rich and had everything a small-man-next-door could want. And the small-man-next-door also had a name which I'm going to start using so that I can stop writing the small-man-next-door.

The name of the small-man-next-door . . . *Drat!* I did it again! Why didn't you stop me?

The name of the s-m-n-d was **Alan**.

Alan didn't have toys or sweets. He had grown-up things like bills and a lawnmower

14

and a moustache. He also had a very tall wife who had very **sproingy hair**. Pam spent a lot of time making her hair **sproingy** and also changing the colour of the **sproings** – red, green, purple, blue, pink. Sometimes she unsproinged her hair for a change and nobody noticed and that made her cross.

While Wilf was peeping at Alan, Wilf's mum came and looked out of the window too.

'Oh goodness. What a lot of stuff they have. I hope they're not going to use our bin,' she said, frowning.

Then Mum told Wilf to go next door and ask Alan if he'd like to come round for tea. She was hoping to broach the subject of the bin.

But Wilf didn't want to go round. He didn't like talking to new people. And his lucky shorts were in the wash. And if Alan came round for tea he might use Wilf's special cup that said 'Wilf' on it. And then Wilf wouldn't want to use it again.

More importantly, while Wilf was peeping out of the window, he had noticed Alan putting a stuffed duck in his hallway. Stuffed animals were on Wilf's **LIST OF THINGS I**

AM OFFICIALLY SCARED OF. He always worried that a stuffed animal was going to strangle him.

Wilf tried to explain this to his mum but she told Wilf not to be *silly* and to go round right away.

Wilf went to his bedroom and got out his shoebox of precious private things. Inside was a leaflet from the library called '**HOW TO STOP WORRYING**'. It had ten suggestions of things to do that might help.

Wilf looked at **NUMBER ONE.**

1) Draw a picture of the thing you are worried about.

Wilf drew a stuffed duck.

NUMBER TWO said:

2) Think of the worst-case scenario.

Wilf thought. What could be worse than being strangled by a stuffed duck? Not much. But possibly being strangled by a stuffed duck that was holding a peanut-butter sandwich.

18

Wilf was scared of getting peanut butter stuck to the roof of his mouth. And it would be worse still if the stuffed duck was wearing a polo-neck jumper. Polo-neck jumpers made Wilf feel all *brahhaaaaahhhoooooeeeuuurrggghhhhh.*

Wilf drew his **WORST-CASE SCENARIO**.

Even looking at the picture made Wilf feel wobbly, so he did a few nonchalant whistles to make himself feel better. And he read on.

NUMBER THREE said:

3) Think of a plan of action if the worst-case scenario happens.

Wilf thought.

If a stuffed duck wearing a polo-neck jumper carrying a peanut-butter sandwich tried to strangle him, he would wear all three of his scarves (which he had knitted himself) to protect his neck. Then he could put the peanut-butter sandwich in a Tupperware box, before catching the duck in a big net.

Wilf drew this.

Then he packed his rucksack with a Tupperware box and a net and wrapped all three of his scarves round his neck. He looked at his leaflet again.

NUMBER FOUR said:

4) *Think of some facts or rational thoughts about the situation.*

Wilf thought and then he wrote down:

* Twenty-two people are injured every year in nightwear incidents
* Half a million people get injured while asleep in bed
* Three million people have to go to hospital every year after accidents at home

* So far there have been no reported incidents of stuffed ducks strangling anyone

So, in fact, Wilf would be safer going round to Alan's house than staying at home.

Wilf took a deep breath, gave Stuart a kiss and popped him in his pocket. It would be all right. *He* would be all right. He wasn't wearing his lucky shorts but he was wearing blue shorts and blue was his third favourite colour. Plus it was a Tuesday and Tuesdays are a sort of bluey colour. And if he took Dot he would be all right because she didn't worry about talking to new people or lucky shorts or special cups.

And *this* was where the whole saving the world shenanigans began . . .

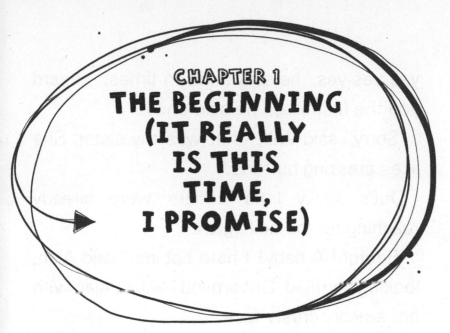

CHAPTER 1
THE BEGINNING (IT REALLY IS THIS TIME, I PROMISE)

Wilf hopped up Alan's path doing one of his special whistles (for good luck).

He rang the bell. And then Dot rang the bell thirteen more times because she liked pressing buttons.

The door flew open. Alan stood there with his hands on his hips, frowning a very frowny frown.

'Yes yes yes yes yes yes yes yes yes yes

yes yes yes,' he said thirteen times. 'I heard you the first time,' he said once.

'Sorry,' said Wilf, 'that was my sister. She likes pressing buttons.'

Dot's sticky little fingers were already reaching for the bell again.

'Eeurgh! A baby! I hate babies!' said Alan, looking horrified. Dot smiled back at Alan with her smeary crusty face.

'She doesn't mean any harm,' said Wilf.

'Eeeurgh! A child! I don't like children either!' said Alan. 'With their irritating skippy little feet and their stupid chirpy little voices and their annoying tufty little hair and their silly puny little bodies,' ranted Alan, pacing up and down in what might have looked, to many, like a silly puny little body.

'Sorry about that,' said Wilf politely.

'And what's that smell?' asked Alan, pulling a face.

'Is it Dot's nappy?' asked Wilf.

'No. It's happiness,' said Alan. 'What do you want?'

'It's just Mum wondered whether you wanted to come round for tea?'

'I'm very busy being evil. Let me introduce myself. I'm Alan,' said Alan, 'and I'm an evil lunatic.'

'Oh, I'm sure you're not,' said Wilf politely. 'I'm sure you're absolutely lovely once people get to know you.'

'No, I'm not,' insisted Alan. 'I'm evil. Not just a little bit evil by accident but properly bigly evil all the time on purpose.'

'You're just being hard on yourself,' said Wilf sympathetically. 'You seem very nice to me.'

'I am *not* nice,' said Alan. 'I'm the baddest, I'm the baddest, I'm the biddly boddly baddest man in the whole wide world and soon everyone will know my name and I will be world-famous for being evil and I will go down in history!'

'Oh,' said Wilf. 'Couldn't you be world-famous in a different way? Like by inventing some kind of really good hoover or something? Or you could enter a talent contest – a lot of people do that these days. What's your favourite song . . . ?'

'Right,' said Alan, 'if you won't believe me, I'm going to have to show you how evil I am.'

Alan picked up Dot, holding her at arm's length.

'This small sticky creature is the perfect size to fire out of my giant bazooka,' said

Alan. 'It will be tremendous fun, although not for her because she'll be splatted and in my experience it's much more fun to be the splatt*er* rather than the splatt*ee*.'

And with that he took Dot inside, slamming the door.

Wilf was staggerblasted. He felt very trembly and his ears went all hot. He felt sick

– but just in his neck – and his knees felt like they might bend the wrong way. What was he going to do? Dot was his sister and although she could be annoying at times he didn't want her to be fired out of a bazooka.

Wilf wanted to run and he wanted to hide and he wanted to cry and he wanted to knit something very elaborate that would take a long time and wouldn't be finished until it was all over. Maybe a jumper for his cuddly octopus.

29

But he didn't do any of those things. He had a great

BIG OLD WORRY

and then he had a great big old think and then he thought so hard that his brain needed a lie-down.

And then he had an idea. He took out the Tupperware box from his rucksack and he stood on it, which was very scary because it was bendy and also it smelt of egg. He stood on tiptoes on the box and he reached and stretched and he found he could *just* about reach the windowsill of the window next to the door.

He clambered up on to the windowsill, which is not easy when your knees keep wanting to go the wrong way. Then he unwrapped all his scarves from his neck, even though it was quite a draughty day, and he tied them all together to make one big long scarf.

He tied one end of the big long scarf to the drainpipe above the window and the other end to his ankle. It meant ruckling his sock right down, and nobody likes a ruckly sock, but this was no time to be stopped by a ruckle.

Wilf scrunched his way through the top of the window, which was a jolly tight squeeze. His pingy ears got flattened to the side of his head and he was worried they might get their crinkles ironed out, but this was no time to be stopped by a crinkle.

Holding the duck net, Wilf lowered himself, in a wibbly wobbly trembly way, into Alan's house.

Meanwhile, Alan was struggling with a large box marked 'Bazooka – This Way Up' which was upside down. Dot was watching him carefully. She took off her sock, wiped her nose and tossed the sock over her shoulder.

Silently, Wilf waggled the net towards Dot. It was like trying to catch a fish. A rather heavy sticky snotty fish with a full nappy.

32

Dot watched with interest
as Wilf swung from his ankle
this way and that, wildly
waving the net. Finally
Dot thought she
saw an interesting-
looking crumb in
the bottom of
the net and she
crawled in.

Yipeedoodledee! thought Wilf. He hauled up his stinky catch, climbed back up the big long scarf and scrunched back through the window.

He landed back on the doorstep and, stopping only to re-crinkle his ears, he ran all the way home with Dot under his arm.

Wilf told his mum that Alan wouldn't be joining them for tea. He didn't mention anything about the kerfuffle with Dot and the bazooka or anything about Alan being an evil lunatic because the whole thing made him feel very scared and like he might faint. So he decided that was the end of it.

But was it?

Yes, it was.

Oh really?

Yes, definitely.

You're really sure that was the end of it?

Absolutely.

Are you though? Are you though? Are you though?

Well . . . *all right*! Maybe it was the end of it apart from the whole world-ending thing. As far as that was concerned, it was still only the *beginning*.

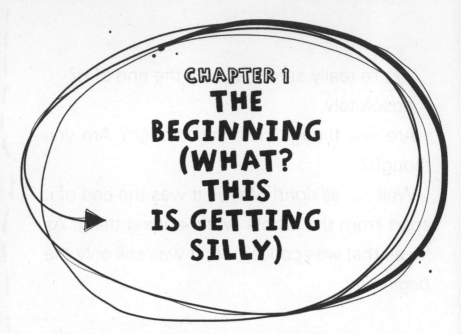

CHAPTER 1
THE BEGINNING (WHAT? THIS IS GETTING SILLY)

Wilf was in bed, hiding, as you do. And trying not to wonder what shenanigans were going on next door. But trying not to wonder is still wondering and so then he started to wonder how he could stop wondering.

Meanwhile, next door, Alan was doing his own wondering. He had started to unpack and he just couldn't decide which room should be his evil lair. Should it be the room with the view of the garden? Or the room with the bay window? Or the little cubby-hole room that was too small for a bed? Or should it be the huge underground lair beneath the house complete with missile-launcher, shark tank and a maze of tunnels leading to a volcano?

Actually, on second thoughts, it was an easy decision. The room with the bay window, of course! But by the time Alan had dragged his **MISSILE LAUNCH CONTROL COMMAND CENTRE CONSOLE** and comfy swivel chair in there, Pam had already bagsied it as her gym. So he had to use the underground lair after all.

Alan moved his belongings into his new evil lair and started wondering where to put his pictures up. It wasn't long before Kevin Phillips turned up. Kevin Phillips was Alan's right-hand man and the mastermind of his evil plans. Every evil lunatic needs a right-hand man because it's a tiring job and you need help with the paperwork.

'What do you think of my evil lair?' Alan asked Kevin.

Kevin was as silent as a wardrobe.

Alan thought this was probably a good sign.

'I thought I'd get some little golf buggies to take us around the underground tunnels.'

Kevin coughed.

'And look, I got you this comfy swivel chair for when you're sitting at the **MISSILE LAUNCH CONTROL COMMAND CENTRE CONSOLE**.

Kevin walked over to the comfy chair and sat on it. Alan could have sworn he saw a smile play over his lips.

Kevin Phillips was the strong silent type. He was as clever as a mushroom and loyal too – but he wasn't much good for a chat.

'I've got this photo I took of a sunset,' said Alan. 'Do you think it looks best here? Or here? Or how about here?'

Kevin looked at Alan long and hard. Then he sighed.

'Maybe I'll put it in the loo,' said Alan meekly. 'You're right. We probably shouldn't be worrying about pictures – we have worlds to destroy. Well, one anyway. So let's get on with it. *This* is the beginning. Of the end!'

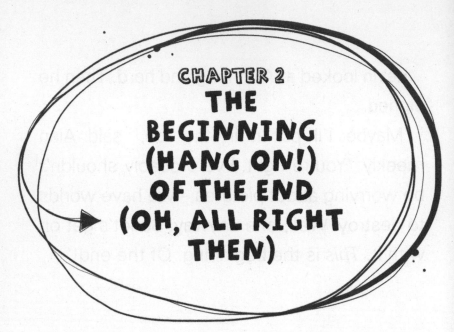

CHAPTER 2
THE BEGINNING (HANG ON!) OF THE END (OH, ALL RIGHT THEN)

The beginning of the end of the world was a lovely sunny day with occasional showers sweeping in from the west.

Wilf was out in his garden playing with Dot. He would throw her a ball, then she would slobber on it for a while, before lobbing it over her shoulder.

Wilf would pick it up, wipe it on a leaf and then the whole game would start again.

Stuart the woodlouse was sunbathing on a Smarties lid.

Meanwhile, Alan was next door in his garden, looking in various boxes.

'I can't find the killer sharks for the shark tank!' he said.

Kevin Phillips looked at Alan quizzically.

'I was sure I'd put them in with my knick-knacks!' Alan kicked a box crossly.

Kevin Phillips chewed on a pen.

'Have you seen them anywhere?' asked Alan, getting exasperated.

Kevin Phillips scratched his chin.

'Nothing's where it's meant to be. I thought I'd put the cushion for the swivel chair in the box marked "Cushions" – but I just found it in a box containing a lamp, two forks and my skipping rope which is all tangled up!'

Kevin Phillips sighed and peered into a box. He pulled out one shoe and placed it on the floor. The other shoe did not appear to be in there. Alan kicked a box again and began trying to untangle his skipping rope.

Just then Alan noticed Wilf and Dot over the fence.

'What are you doing there?' asked Alan. 'Didn't the security guards wrestle you to the ground the moment they saw you?'

'No, because we're in our own garden,' said Wilf reasonably.

'Not for long,' said Alan. 'I'm going to buy

your garden and flatten it and pave it over so that I can park my hover tank there.'

'What's a hover tank?' asked Wilf.

ORPHAN SIGHS

'It's basically a huge tank that hovers over the ground.'

'Wow!' said Wilf. 'That sounds amazing!'

'It is,' said Alan. 'It is powered by the sighs of orphans. A thousand sighs needed per second for fuel,' he added proudly.

'Couldn't you just use air?' asked Wilf.

'No!' said Alan. 'Because, because . . . because I'm just a bit busy untangling my skipping rope at the moment if you don't

mind thank you very much.'

Alan wrestled with his skipping rope and made it a bit more tangly and also made the bobbly end fall off. He sighed and put the bobble in the bin.

'That's actually *our bin*,' said a small muffled voice from inside Wilf's house.

'Is it all right if we play in our own garden until you flatten it?' asked Wilf politely. 'It's just I promised my mum that I'd mow the lawn.'

Alan snorted pityingly. 'Mow the lawn? I have a robot who does that for me. Maybe I should ask him to do it today. It's a nice day for it.'

'What did you say?' asked Wilf.

'It's a nice day for it,' repeated Alan.

'No, no, before that – the thing about the robot!' prompted Wilf.

'Oh yeah. *That*,' said Alan in rather a showy-off way. 'I've built myself a robot – to do my *every bidding*. Which is just a posh way of saying "do whatever I blinking well say".'

'Gosh!' said Wilf, impressed. 'That sounds brilliant!'

'Would you like to see him?' asked Alan.

Wilf wasn't sure that he did. Alan did seem a bit evil, after all, what with the bazooka and everything. But he also seemed lonely,

and Wilf knew what it was like to feel lonely.
Wilf's mum was always telling him to try to be
more friendly, so Wilf decided to give it a go.

'OK,' said Wilf bravely. 'Yes.'

Alan led Wilf and Dot to a shed. He opened
the door. Shafts of light filtered through the
dark, poking at the gloom and
annoying it a bit. There was a
dusty musty fusty smell.

'Let me introduce you to the **LRX2FL309VERSION8.4MARKIII**,' said Alan grandly.

Wilf peered through the shadows and could

just make out a large great big robot with legs and arms and a face and everything.

'Wow!' said Wilf again. 'What do you call him?'

'I call him LRX2FL309version8.4markIII,' said Alan, looking at Wilf as though he was a little bit of an idiot.

'Why don't you call him Mark III? For short?'

Alan stared at Wilf for a long time. Then he turned to the robot and said, 'Mark III? I've brought someone to meet you.'

The robot didn't move.

'What can he do?' asked Wilf.

'Anything I want him to,' said Alan proudly.

'Wow! Get him to do something!' said Wilf excitedly.

'OK,' said Alan.

Wilf looked at Alan expectantly.

Alan cleared his throat.

'Mark III?' he called.

The robot didn't move.

'Mark III?' said Alan more loudly.

Nothing.

'Mark III!!!!' shouted Alan.

The robot stirred.

'Hmm? Wha . . . ? Whassup?' said the robot sleepily.

'I'd like you to tidy up in here, please,' said Alan.

'GO AWAY. I'm asleep,' said the robot in a strange whiny voice that changed from very high-pitched to very low-pitched from one word to the next.

'Mark III . . .' said Alan with a hint of warning in his voice.

'I tidied it, like, three months ago. Leave me *alone*. You're *always* nagging me,' said the robot.

'He normally does whatever I ask him to,' said Alan, a little embarrassed. 'I probably programmed him wrongly. I just need to make a few adjustments . . .'

'I'm sure it's amazing when he *does* do whatever you ask him to,' said Wilf kindly.

'Yeah. It would be,' said Alan a little wistfully.

Wilf and Dot and Alan tiptoed out of the shed. Kevin Phillips was waiting in the garden, holding a newspaper. He did not look pleased to see them.

'I've been looking for you everywhere,' said Alan. 'Where have you been?'

Kevin sniffed and stared coolly at Wilf and Dot.

'Forget about them, we have things to do. Come on.'

Kevin Phillips ignored Alan and headed briskly for the kitchen.

'All right, well, when you've had something to eat, come to the evil lair,' said Alan.

Alan tutted to himself. 'He leaves me to do all the work on the

SECRET EVIL PLAN

and he's *meant* to be my right-hand man. Which means he's *meant* to help.'

'What **secret evil plan**?' asked Wilf.

'Have I told you that **I'm the baddest, the**

baddest, the biddly boddly baddest in the whole wide world?'

'Yes, you did mention that,' said Wilf. 'But you didn't tell me about a **secret evil plan**.'

'That's because it's - - -,

- - - - - - - - - -

▶ a **secret**,' said Alan.

Alan was good at keeping secrets. When I say good I mean bad. And when I say secrets I mean guinea pigs. Alan was bad at keeping guinea pigs. They were always dying or escaping.

55

Come to think of it, he wasn't much good at keeping secrets either. So it wasn't very long (about forty-eight seconds) before he had blurted out his whole

SECRET EVIL PLAN.

56

'I,' he said. 'I, Alan,' he repeated for effect. 'I, Alan, myself, have a secret evil plan that nobody knows and that secret evil plan is to totally and utterly and **completely destroy the world** until it is destroyed. Because,' said Alan, 'as **I may have mentioned, I'm the baddest, I'm the baddest, I'm the biddly boddly baddest man in the whole wide worlderoony.'**

Luckily for Alan, Kevin Phillips was out of earshot, so he didn't hear Alan blurting out their **secret evil plan**, because if he had heard, he would have been **piping cross**.

Once Wilf had heard Alan's **evil plan** he was absolutely staggerblasted.

THE WORLD? DESTROYED? FOREVER?

That could only be a bad thing. Wilf knew he had to be stopped. And Wilf knew he had to be the one to do the stopping. It was time for him to do something heroic.

Or actually, on second thoughts, was it time to hide under the duvet and whistle and pretend none of this had ever happened? Somehow that sounded like a better option.

CHAPTER 3
WILF SAVES THE WORLD

Wilf hid and whistled and whistled and hid. He did a bit of knitting. Then some more whistling and hiding. He gave Stuart the woodlouse a bit of a runaround. And as he watched Stuart trotting about in a carefree way, the wind in his legs, the sun on his back, playing football with the pink hundred and thousand Wilf had saved for him – Wilf realized something.

He couldn't hide in bed and whistle and pretend everything was fine. It *wasn't* fine. And for the sake of Stuart and Dot and lots of other people and woodlouses (woodlice? Woodlii?) everywhere, he had to

something. He had to save the day. And the world. Both. At the same time. He needed to get to Alan's evil lair and find out *how* he was going to destroy the world and with *what*.

There was just one problem. The only way to get to Alan's evil lair was in a lift. And Wilf was scared of lifts. In particular, Wilf was scared of getting stuck in a lift and suffocating.

Wilf drew a picture of this.

Then he thought about what could be worse than being stuck in a lift.

The only thing that could be worse was if there was a giant moth in the lift. Wilf was really scared of moths.

Wilf had a great **BIG OLD WORRY**. Then he had a great big old think. He thought and thought. He thought so hard that his brain needed a lie-down. And then he had an idea.

If he took a torch, that would attract the moth to the torch, instead of to him. Then, if he sprayed the moth with hairspray, its wings would go stiff and it wouldn't be able to flutter in that scary way. And if Wilf took a little bag of air with him, he might not suffocate in the lift.

Wilf drew this.

He packed his rucksack with a torch and hairspray and a little bag of air. Then he looked at the '**HOW TO STOP WORRYING**' leaflet again.

NUMBER FIVE said:

5) Sometimes it helps to distract yourself by thinking of something completely different.

That was a good idea. Wilf decided to think of words that began with 's'.

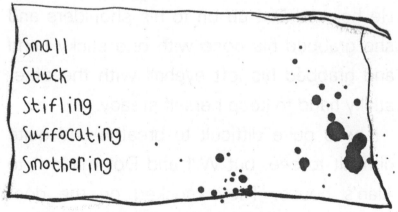

Small
Stuck
Stifling
Suffocating
Smothering

No, no, no. That wasn't helping!
Something else. He decided to think of

words that begin with 'f'.

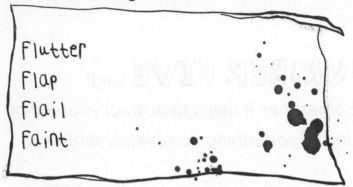

Flutter
Flap
Flail
Faint

No, no, no! That was making it worse!

Wilf decided he'd better just get on with it. He hoicked Dot up on to his shoulders and she grabbed his nose with one sticky hand and grabbed his left eyeball with the other sticky hand to keep herself steady.

It was quite difficult to breathe and quite difficult to see, but Wilf and Dot made it to Alan's house. They knocked on the door and then hid behind a bush. While Alan was looking for who had knocked on the door, they tiptoed into the house.

Wilf took a deep breath and pressed the button for the lift.

The lift doors opened.

The good news was: *no giant moth*.

The bad news was: *a big security guard*.

Wilf briefly wondered whether he had time to go to the loo before confronting the security guard – but decided he didn't. He sprayed the hairspray in the guard's eyes. The guard screamed and fell out of the lift. Wilf and Dot stepped in and pressed the button marked

EVIL LAIR.

The lift doors closed. Wilf took a little sip of air from his bag of extra air.

The lift started going down.

DOWN

DOWN

DOWN

DOWN
DOWN
DOWN
DOWN
DOWN
DOWN
DOWN
DOWN
DOWN
DOWN
DOWN
DOWN
DOWN
DOWN
DOWN
DOWN
DOWN
STOP

The doors opened again.

Wilf had done it! He had been in a lift and it hadn't got stuck! He did a hoppy dance of joy. And then he put the torch in between the doors so that they wouldn't close and the lift would stay there and they would have a quick getaway.

Wilf and Dot tiptoed to the corner of the evil

lair and crouched down, as quiet as cushions.

Wilf was staggerblasted at what he saw. There were screens and buttons and more buttons and a lot more screens and tunnels and golf buggies and rather a nice picture of a sunset.

It was all really swishy-swoo.

'Wow!' whispered Wilf.

'You like it?' asked Alan, who was standing right behind him.

Wilf jumped out of his skin. 'H-h-how did you know I was here?' he stammered.

'That smell,' said Alan.

'Oh. Happiness?' asked Wilf.

'No. I think it's your sister's nappy.'

Dot was crawling quickly across the floor, leaving a trail of crispies and raisins behind her.

'Oh,' said Wilf. 'Yes. It could be that.'

Dot had spotted an enormous blanky and was heading straight for it.

'It seems she is just in time to unveil my new weapon. Behold!' said Alan dramatically as Dot pulled at the corner of the giant blanky and revealed a great big large enormous shiny metal gun-shaped thing.

Wilf stared up in amazement.

'I'm going to call it my

Weapon for
EXTREME EXTERMINATION
AND WORLD-ENDING EXPERIMENTS –

or **WEE-WEE** for short,' said Alan.

Wilf couldn't help giggling.

'What?' said Alan. 'Oh drat. Hmmm. All right, I'm going to call it my

WEAPON OF
INTERNATIONAL AND
NATIONAL KILLING
AND EXTERMINATION
ENTERPRISES – or my **WINKEE** for short.'

Wilf tried ever so hard not to laugh but he

couldn't help a quick splutter.

'What now?' said Alan crossly. 'Oh, I *see*. Hang on then. Let me think . . .'

Alan paced about. 'How about my **POWERFUL ALL-NUCLEAR TERROR SYSTEM**.

Yes! That's it! Just wait till I unleash the true horror of my **PANTS!**'

Wilf chuckled into his sleeve.

Alan sighed. 'I've done it again, haven't I?' he said forlornly.

'Yes,' said Wilf, 'but don't worry. Why don't you just call it your **Big Gun Thingy** and we'll all know what you mean.'

'OK, thanks,' said Alan. 'And now, if you'll excuse me, I have a world to destroy.'

'How are you going to do that?' asked Wilf casually, as though it were no big deal.

72

'Well, not long from now, all the world leaders are meeting in London to practise shaking hands with each other. While they are all distracted, I shall destroy the world with my **Big Gun Thingy**!'

'How will you get to London?' asked Wilf, always practical.

'I'm glad you asked me that,' said Alan proudly. 'I am building a **most magnificent most marvellous most magical mechanical flying machine**. Let me show you . . .'

But before Alan could show Wilf his new invention, they were interrupted by Kevin Phillips rushing into the room and skidding across the shiny floor.

'Don't worry, I have apprehended the intruders,' said Alan to Kevin Phillips.

Kevin Phillips approached Wilf and sniffed.

'It's the girl's nappy. Don't worry. They will both soon be dead,' said Alan.

Kevin Phillips growled menacingly at Wilf, then turned on his heels and sat down in the comfy swivel chair at the **Missile Launch Control Command Centre Console**.

Alan suddenly remembered his manners.

'Wilf, you've met Kevin Phillips, haven't you? He's my right-hand man. And mastermind of my evil plans.'

'He's a dog,' said Wilf.

Wilf was not one to mince around the bush.

'I beg your pardon?' said Alan.

'He's a dog,' repeated Wilf, pointing at Kevin Phillips.

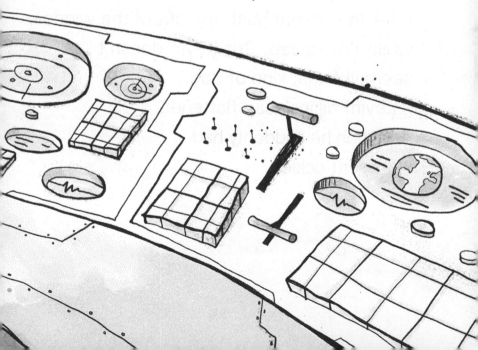

Kevin Phillips barked and swivelled a couple of times on his comfy swivel chair and then sat down again. His tongue lolled out of his mouth and his big tail wagged happily, occasionally bashing against a lever and setting a missile off.

'He's a big shaggy dog,' said Wilf. 'Normally I'm scared of dogs,' he continued, 'because I think they might push me out of the window while I'm asleep. But Kevin doesn't seem like that kind of dog.'

Kevin Phillips's ears flattened. And then he suddenly had an urgent tickle.

'Shhhh!' said Alan, very embarrassed. 'He doesn't know he's a dog. He thinks he's one of us.'

'Sorry,' said Wilf.

'Besides, is it fair that a dog shouldn't have the same rights as a human? The right to go to school and go to the cinema and go bowling and have a job. And the right to destroy the world?'

'Bowling could be difficult,' said Wilf.

'OK, forget the bowling,' said Alan. 'But the other stuff.'

'Well, I suppose . . .' said Wilf.

'You see!' said Alan.

Kevin Phillips barked excitedly and jumped up on to the control panel, setting off another half-dozen missiles.

'Anyway,' said Alan. 'No time to chat. I must get on with killing you and your smelly sister. Dungeon or shark tank?'

'The thing is,' said Wilf, feeling a bit trembly, 'I'm not very good with dark places. Or damp places. Damp makes me cough.'

'Shark tank then.'

'The problem is,' explained Wilf, trying not to let his knees go the wrong way, 'I'm not very good with water. Or sharks.'

'Dungeon then,' said Alan.

78

CHAPTER 4
OH NO, HE DOESN'T

Alan led Wilf and Dot down some steep slimy stairs to a small dark dungeon. It was as cold as a wellington down there. There were no sharks but I bet there were spiders. And probably snails. And lots of things that brushed against your face and made you go *yarhargarhahhhhhherggggggggggggaaaa*. And also another nice photo of a sunset.

Wilf was scared. He really, really didn't like

 79

those long creepy-crawlies with zillions of legs. Or those other ones with waggly wavy feeler things instead of eyes. And he suspected the dungeon was full of wiggly legs and waggly wavers. He didn't mind Stuart the woodlouse because Stuart didn't have waggly wavers and he had a reasonable number of legs. Plus he was always kind and polite.

'Is there a third option?' Wilf asked Alan, sidling towards the doorway. 'Like dungeon, shark tank OR trip to the zoo?'

'No,' said Alan. He stepped in front of Wilf and folded his arms, looking as serious and determined as a chest of drawers.

'Right. Well. Hang on then,' said Wilf. 'I just need to do something.'

He got out his pencil and his notebook and drew the thing that was worrying him:

80

a looooong creepy-crawly.

Alan sighed and tapped his foot impatiently.

Wilf considered the **WORST-CASE SCENARIO**. What could be worse than a looooong creepy-crawly?

Wilf was really scared of wigs. And terrified of roller skates. A looooong creepy-crawly wearing a wig on roller skates?

Wilf drew just that.

Wilf needed a plan to escape the horror of the dungeon.

He thought. And he thought and he thought.

'Come on, come on,' said Alan, jangling his dungeon keys.

'If you're going to leave someone to die, I believe it's traditional to offer them a last meal,' Wilf said finally.

'I've been slaving away all day trying to get this world destroyed and now you expect me to cook you dinner as well?' said Alan.

'It's only polite,' said Wilf quietly.

'All right, all right,' said Alan crossly. 'What do you want?'

'A jar of treacle,' said Wilf. 'And some chopsticks to eat it with.'

'What?' said Alan.

'You're allowed to ask for whatever you like,'

explained Wilf. 'Those are the rules.'

Alan tutted and sighed and said, 'It will ruin your teeth,' but he trotted off and brought back a jar of treacle and some chopsticks.

'Goodbye forever,' he said, pushing Wilf and Dot inside the dungeon.

Kevin Phillips licked Wilf's ear and skidded round on his bottom a bit and then they closed the big door to the dungeon with a

crrrrrrreeeeeeooooonnnnkkkk and turned the key with a *shlonk*.

Wilf and Dot were all alone. Apart from the spiders. And the snails. And those funny long creepy-crawlies with zillions of legs. And those other ones with waggly wavy things coming out of their heads. So, in fact, they weren't alone at all. But in many ways, Wilf and Dot rather wished they were.

It was very dark. And the damp was making Wilf cough. And they were going to die. And then the world was going to end. Or possibly the other way round.

Wilf was as sorry as a sausage. Sorry he'd ever laid eyes on Alan. Sorry he'd ever snuck into the evil lair. And very sorry he'd not worn thicker socks because his feet were like blocks of ice.

But he had a plan. A creepy-crawly plan. You see, he wasn't really going to eat the treacle with chopsticks. If any wig-wearing creepy-crawly rolled towards him on roller skates, he was going to tip the treacle in front of it so that the roller skates got stuck. Then he was going to use the chopsticks to remove the wig. *Simple.*

Wilf took out the leaflet on **'HOW TO STOP WORRYING'** from his pocket.

NUMBER SIX said:

6) *It can be helpful to rate your fear out of ten.*

Wilf thought. If he had to rate his fear he would say it was a

BIG BIG

number. Like about a

KERBILLION.

A bit like the number of legs those long creepy-crawlies have. Horrid wiggly waggly legs. Billions of them. *Aaargh.*

Rating his fear was just making Wilf feel worse. And reminding him of the wiggly waggly legs. And also reminding him that he was also scared of maths.

What would make Wilf feel better would be

if he could get out of the dungeon and away from the weird wig-wearing waggly pests skating around in the dark.

Wilf had a great **big old worry**. Then he had a great big old think. And he thought and thought until his brain needed a lie-down. And then he had an idea.

He opened his jar of treacle and he poured it over his drawing.

He slid the paper under the door of the dungeon.

Then he got a chopstick and poked it through the keyhole, knocking the key out of the other side of the door. It dropped with a splat on to

the treacle-covered paper – and it stuck fast. Wilf pulled the paper back under the door and retrieved the key.

He gave the key to Dot and she licked it clean in a few seconds. Wilf put it into the lock, turned the key with a *schlonk* – and then with two bounds they were free!

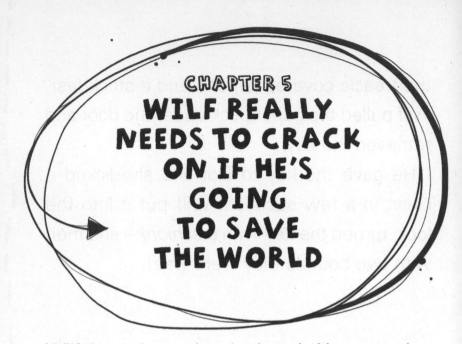

CHAPTER 5
WILF REALLY NEEDS TO CRACK ON IF HE'S GOING TO SAVE THE WORLD

Wilf tiptoed past the shark tank. He was going to stop that evil lunatic (and his right-hand dog). And he was going to save the world. Then, and only then, would he change into a pair of thicker socks.

But just as he was creeping slowly and silently towards the door leading out of the evil lair, he heard a loud *badoinking* sound. Suddenly the door flew open and MarkIII came galumphing in. He threw himself on the comfy swivel chair and ate a loaf of bread. Wilf hid behind a large sculpture of a small person. Or it might have been a small sculpture of a very tall person. It was hard to tell.

Alan beamed at the robot.

'At last!' he said. 'Where have you been?'

'Out,' said the robot.

'I need you to do something for me. I need you to invade Russia,' said Alan grandly, clasping his fist and holding it in the air. It was a new thing that he thought made him look more evil.

'Yeah, I'm not really in the mood for invading Russia,' croaked Mark III.

'I don't care whether you're in the mood,' said Alan. 'I'm asking you to do it so I want you to do it.'

'But I'm *busy*,' said the robot.

'Busy?' said Alan. 'Doing what? Staring out of the window?'

'Yeah. And also, might meet up with some friends later.'

'There aren't even any windows in here! And you can meet up with your friends once you've invaded Russia,' said Alan.

'Why me? I don't even know where Russia is!'

'Don't know where Russia is?!' said Alan, hopping from foot to foot with rage. 'I spent a billion pounds on you! I spent seven years inputting information. You *do* know where Russia is! It's on your hard drive!'

'Is it . . . abroad?' asked Mark III.

'Is it abroad?' raged Alan, his voice going all squeaky. 'Is it abroad? Of course it's abroad! Please tell me you knew it was abroad? All those years! All that money! Why did I bother?'

Alan pounded his tiny fists on his desk and sobbed. This didn't make him look more evil, it just made him look a bit sad. Wilf leaned out from behind the statue and passed him a tissue. Not a clean one – it was the one that he had just used to wipe Dot's face – but even so.

As Alan blew his nose, Mark III ambled out of the evil lair just as Kevin Phillips was on his way in.

Kevin Phillips looked from Alan to Mark III and then back to Alan again.

'Don't say it,' said Alan.

Kevin Phillips said nothing.

'I know what you're thinking,' said Alan. 'But he's *my* Mark III. My one and only Mark III.'

Kevin Phillips sighed.

'I know, I know,' said Alan. 'But one day he'll come good.'

Kevin Phillips didn't look convinced.

'He will!' said Alan. 'And one day he'll take over from me and he'll need a right-hand man. He'll need you. You're the best right-hand man an evil lunatic could have.'

Alan and Kevin Phillips hugged each other and Alan cried a bit more and Wilf pretended he was very interested in the curtains because he felt he shouldn't be there.

And then he remembered he really SHOULDN'T be there. They'd captured him and he was actually meant to be escaping right now as a matter of fact thank you very much!

Wilf scooped up Dot in his arms and made his way back to the lift without making a single sound.

Well, except for the sound of Dot saying, 'Bye-bye, bye-bye, weevil woonatic,' about eighteen times. Luckily Alan and Kevin Phillips were too busy hugging and crying and patting each other to notice.

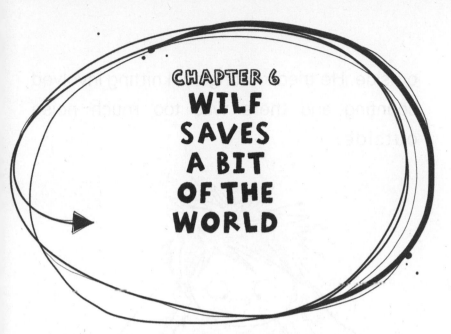

CHAPTER 6
WILF
SAVES
A BIT
OF THE
WORLD

Wilf was back under his duvet. He couldn't stop thinking about what he had discovered next door. Alan had a **most magnificent most marvellous most magical mechanical flying machine**. And a **Big Gun Thingy**. And he was going to use one to get to London and the other to destroy the world. Meep!

Wilf tried to take his mind off it all by whistling, but there was too much noise outside. He tried knitting but knitting involved counting and there was too much noise outside.

He tried just lying there and thinking about happy things like gerbils dressed up as famous historical figures – but there was too much noise outside. Wilf decided to get up and see what all the noise was.

Looking out of the landing window, Wilf could see Alan in his garden, working on his most **magnificent most marvellous most magical mechanical flying machine**. He couldn't quite see what it looked like because it was covered by a sheet and surrounded by a fence.

Alan was hammering very loudly on nails and every so often his thumb. Occasionally

Alan would drop his hammer and Kevin Phillips would pick it up and run and hide it behind an old plant pot and then bark excitedly. And Alan would have to climb down his ladder to fetch it.

Wilf did a **big old worry**, and his stomach tried to do a somersault but it tripped and just did a sort of *flobberdy splat*, and his knees tried to go the wrong way – because Wilf knew that once Alan finished his **most magnificent most marvellous most magical mechanical flying machine** he would fly to London and then he would destroy the world. And that could only be a *bad thing*.

Wilf tiptoed out into the garden. If he could just get to the flying machine . . .

'Right,' said Alan to Kevin Phillips, 'let's lock

the fence and make sure nobody can get to the flying machine.'

Drat, thought Wilf. But if he could just find a way of unlocking the fence . . .

'Then we must get some lions to guard the fence so that nobody can unlock it,' continued Alan.

Double drat, thought Wilf.

'But first,' said Alan grandly, 'I am going to carry out **phase one** of my evil plan. The thing is, Kevin, there's only one world. So you only get to destroy it once. And I don't want to make a hash of it and end up looking silly. So in order to practise destroying the world, I am going to test out my **Big Gun Thingy** on a small patch of world – namely a tiny island called Wyland Island.'

Wilf gasped. Wyland Island? That was

where his auntie lived and where he and Dot went on school holidays. He couldn't let anything happen to Wyland Island! It was only the best place *ever*, with a really whizzy slide and very diggy sand and an ice-cream van that sold blue ice cream.

Not only that, Wyland Island was a very important *historical* island. It was invaded by people from the north in the eighteen hundreds and not long afterwards was invaded by people from the south.

After a long and bloody battle that lasted well over twenty minutes, the two peoples had come to a truce and lived peacefully side by side. But they had insisted on having all the signs on the island in their own language. Just to be difficult.

Why on earth would anyone choose to destroy Wyland Island? wondered Wilf.

'You are probably wondering why I have chosen to destroy Wyland Island,' said Alan to Kevin.

To be honest, Kevin looked more like he was wondering why his ear wouldn't stop tickling. But Alan continued nevertheless.

'I chose Wyland Island because it is small, it is nearby and it has a very good knick-knack shop near where you get off the ferry,' said Alan.

This was all true. Wilf could not fault him on his reasoning.

'I am not going to take you with me, Kevin Phillips, because swishy tails and small knick-knack shops are not a good combination,' said Alan. 'So you stay here. Stay. Sit. Stay. Kevin, stay. I said *stay*. Kevin!'

But Kevin had gone to bark at a tree for half an hour because he thought he *might* have seen a squirrel.

Alan sighed, picked up his **Big Gun Thingy** and set off for Wyland Island on his own.

But he wasn't on his own, was he?

Because Wilf, stopping only to brush his teeth, comb his hair, pop Stuart in his pocket and put Dot in her buggy, was *right behind him*.

Wilf chased silently after Alan. Down the

street, up the road, down the lane, up the alley – straight to the port.

Oh no! The port! The port meant boats. And boats meant sea. And sea meant that anxious wobbly feeling in Wilf's tummy. What if there were sea monsters? What if there was a giant squid? Or even a normal-sized squid? Or a jellyfish? Or a prawn – they had waggly things and scary little eyes. Wilf wanted to tiptoe right home again. No one need ever know he'd been there. But *he* would know.

Wilf got out his pencil and notebook and drew what he was worried about.

A sea monster sinking the ferry.

And then he drew the **WORST-CASE**

SCENARIO.

A sea monster with a twirly moustache sinking the ferry and then eating Wilf and Dot. Wilf was scared of twirly moustaches. And of being eaten.

Wilf had a great **big old worry**. Then he

had a great big old think. And he thought and thought until his brain needed a lie-down.

He looked at Dot and she smiled back, a

snotty crusty smile. And she sneezed.

And then it hit him – not the snot, the idea.

When Wilf and Dot were at home and Dot was crawling towards Wilf and Wilf was worried she was going to snot on his knees, he would throw a raisin to distract her.

So if sea monsters worked the same way as Dot, he just needed to do a bigger version of the raisin trick.

Wilf rushed to the shop and bought two pairs of goggles (in case the ferry was sunk by a sea monster), a small pair of scissors (for moustache-snipping) and a large Christmas pudding, because it looked like a great big ball of raisins.

Delicious.

Wilf was sure the sea monster would like it.

IT WAS A GOOD PLAN.

IT WAS A GREAT PLAN.
I'VE GOT NOTHING AGAINST THE PLAN.

But while Wilf was shopping, Alan went and bought the very last ticket for the twelve o'clock ferry. *Drat.* What was Wilf going to do now? The next ferry wasn't for *three* hours.

It was the perfect opportunity to go home and hide in bed.

But what good would that do?

It would make Wilf feel a whole lot better for a start.

Yes, but only in the short term.

So what? That's better than nothing.

Hang on, excuse me, who are you? I'm telling the story. Stop butting in and disagreeing with me.

Sorry.

So where was I . . . ?

109

I won't say anything else.

Good.

Wilf got out his **'HOW TO STOP WORRYING'** leaflet.

NUMBER SEVEN said:

7) *Try thinking positive thoughts.*

This was a good idea. Wilf thought and thought. And he thought. And he thought that he should be brave and catch the next ferry. And that there probably *wasn't* such a thing as sea monsters. And if there *was* such a

thing as sea monsters, they might be friendly. And if they *weren't* friendly, they might not be hungry. And if they *were* hungry, they might not like the taste of small boys called Wilf. Or they might be allergic to small boys called Wilf. All very **positive** thoughts. Feeling very **positive**, Wilf bought his ticket and waited.

Chug chug chug chug went Alan.

Stand stand stand stand went Wilf, Dot and Stuart (waiting for the ferry).

Chug chug chug chug went Alan.

Stand stand stand stand went Wilf, Dot and Stuart.

Chug chug chug chug went Alan.

This is a rubbish chase, thought Wilf.

Finally, Wilf, Dot and Stuart got on the next ferry.

Chug chug chug chug went Alan – in the

distance.

Chug chug went Wilf, very very slowly, because he was on the slower ferry.

Chug chug chug chug went Alan, almost out of sight.

Chug chug went Wilf, watching as a piece of driftwood overtook them.

'I'll have the little china robin standing on a china twig,' went Alan – because by now he was in the knick-knack shop.

Chug chug went Wilf.

Four hours later, they reached Wyland Island.

Wilf hadn't been sick and he hadn't seen a squid (giant or otherwise) or a sea monster or a prawn. It had been fine! He wasn't scared of boats any more! Hooray!

Wilf did a little hoppy dance of celebration and then thought that perhaps he should hurry up and catch Alan. So he did hopping on two legs which some people call running but it's much more **sproingy**.

By the time Wilf caught up with Alan, Alan had already announced the first stage of his world- destroying plans, and an angry mob had formed.

I wouldn't be exaggerating if I said there were at least two of them.

The rest were at home because they didn't like confrontation.

'Do not destroy our island!' shouted one.

'Do not destroy our island!' shouted the other, in his own, different, language.

'What did he just say?' said the first one, to no one in particular.

'I can't understand a word you're saying,' said the second one to the first.

'Why don't you let me translate?' suggested Wilf.

'Good idea,' said the first one. Let's call him Bob.

'Good idea,' said the second one. Let's call him Bob too. No, hang on, that's a silly idea. Let's call him Horatio.

'Good idea,' said Alan. 'Right, everyone. The good news is: I'm about to try out my latest state-of-the-art high-tech swizzy whizzy **Big Gun Thingy**. The bad news is: it will involve destroying your island and everything on it and, in many ways, *you*.'

Wilf turned to Bob and said, 'I'm afraid you're all going to die.'

Then he turned to Horatio and said, 'I'm afraid you're all going to die.'

Bob and Horatio clutched their chests, clutched their mouths, clutched each other.

'**Noooooooooooooooooooooooooo!**' said Bob.

'**Noooooooooooooooooooooooooo!**' said Horatio.

'We must, how you say, stop him!' said Bob to Horatio.

Horatio got a small phrase book out of his pocket and looked up the word 'yes'. It was 'yes'.

'Yes,' said Horatio.

'Too late!' said Alan. 'Because all I have to do is to tap in a code here . . .'

Alan tapped in a series of numbers which were actually his birthday plus his age.

'. . . and then aim the **Big Gun Thingy** at you, and the entire island will evaporate in a billion-degree meltdown. So brace yourself because this may sting a little . . .'

Alan's finger moved towards the

FIRE

button.

It was as if everything was happening in slow motion. In fact, Alan was just doing it really slowly for dramatic effect.

As his finger moved slowly, slowly, slowly towards the button, Wilf had a great idea. He reached into his rucksack, got out the Christmas pudding and rolled it down the barrel of the Big Gun Thingy just as Alan pressed the

button.

The pudding was an exact fit.

There was a pause. Wilf looked at Alan. Alan looked at Wilf. Bob looked at Horatio. Horatio looked at Bob. They all looked at each other.

What had Wilf done? Had he stopped the **Big Gun Thingy**? Wilf put Dot's goggles on Dot and his goggles on himself.

Time stood still. Then time shuffled about a bit and kicked a stone. Then time carried on again.

There was a rumble. And a whirr. And a sort of gulp and then the laser flashed out across the island, plunging everything into a ghastly red light for several seconds.

Suddenly Bob and Horatio and Alan started screaming. They slapped their heads and hopped about and ran in circles. But they didn't melt.

Wilf's Christmas pudding had absorbed almost all of the Big Gun Thingy's power and had reduced the setting from Billion Degree Meltdown to Smouldering Eyebrows. And now all six of their eyebrows were smouldering away. (Luckily, Stuart didn't have eyebrows, and Wilf's and Dot's were protected by their goggles, for the eyebrow-counters among you.)

Bob cuffed Horatio. Horatio threw a bucket of water over Bob. Wilf very kindly thwacked Alan's forehead with Dot's pig.

In a matter of seconds their eyebrows had stopped smouldering and all was quiet. Although there was an odd burnt-eyebrowy kind of smell in the air.

'Thank you!' said Bob to Wilf.

'Thank you!' said Horatio to Wilf.

'Typical!' said Alan to Wilf.

'You saved everything!' said Bob.

'You ruined everything!' said Alan.

'We're alive!' said Horatio joyfully.

'They're alive!' said Alan irritably. 'I'm not going to go down in the **history books** for just smouldering a couple of people's eyebrows, am I?' he said forlornly.

'Look,' said Wilf sympathetically, 'I think it's time to go home. I think you're a little bit tired.'

'I am *not* tired!' said Alan, yawning and rubbing his eyes.

'And emotional,' said Wilf.

'Waaaaaaaaah, I'm not emooootionnnnalllllll,' said Alan, bursting into tears.

'And you know how that always makes you bad-tempered,' said Wilf.

'WHAT?' yelled Alan. 'I am NOT bad-tempered! How DARE you say I am bad-tempered? That makes me so ANGRY when people say I am bad-tempered because it's JUST NOT TRUE!' said Alan, pounding his angry little fists on the ground.

'I am NOT tired, I am wide AWAKE and I . . .'

Alan was asleep.

Wilf put Dot's blanky over him. He picked her up, checked Stuart was still in his pocket, and tiptoed away with Bob and Horatio.

Bob followed the sign saying 'Town Centre' and Horatio followed a different sign saying 'Town Centre' and Wilf and Dot followed the sign saying –'Ferry'.

FERRY
FERRY

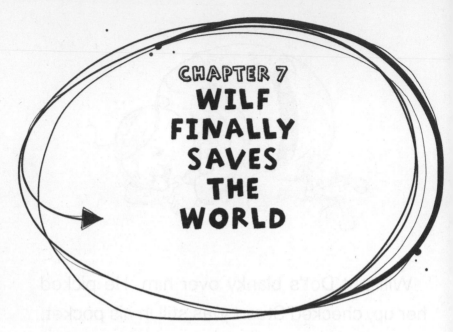

CHAPTER 7
WILF FINALLY SAVES THE WORLD

It was lunchtime and Wilf was in the kitchen. He was eating a sandwich with relish. By which I mean he was enjoying it. But, come to think of it, his sandwich was cheese with relish. So in fact he was eating his sandwich with relish with relish.

And he was thinking that after the whole Wyland Island kerfuffle, maybe life would go back to normal. He'd saved a little bit of the

124

world – maybe now he could learn a new whistle or hone his hop or knit a new outfit for Stuart the woodlouse. Maybe Alan would stay on Wyland Island and stop being evil and take up ballroom dancing.

Wilf chewed happily, watching Dot while she carefully placed a slice of cheese in the DVD machine. Then she stood up and started to smear a second slice of cheese on the window.

As Wilf was watching, he noticed something behind the smear. It was Alan getting off the bus with his Big Gun Thingy. He did not look happy and he did not look like he had taken up ballroom dancing. He marched up to his own front door and rang the bell. No reply. He rang again. No reply. He hammered on the door and shouted, 'LRX2FL309version8.4markIII! Wake up!'

Nothing.

Wilf slipped off his chair and went outside. He was just about to ask Alan whether he wanted to wait in their house when Alan's door opened. Mark III stood there blinking. Kevin Phillips jumped up at Alan excitedly and put his muddy paws all over his anorak.

'What's going on?' said Mark III. 'What time is it?'

'It's time to destroy the world!' said Alan. 'Today's the day! Step one – you invade China. Step two – you round everyone up and tell them to stand still. Step three – I arrive with my Big Gun Thingy and then we destroy the—'

'Yeah, I'm still not so sure about this whole world-destroying thing . . .' said Mark III.

'What?' said Alan.

'I've gone off it,' said Mark III.

'But, but, but . . . it's all arranged and paid for!' said Alan, bewildered.

'Yeah. I think I'm going to go travelling instead.'

'Well, could you *travel* to China,' suggested Alan hopefully, 'and then destroy it?'

'I was thinking of somewhere more beachy,' said Mark III.

'*OK*,' said Alan. 'Well, in that case, could you travel to somewhere more *beachy* – and then destroy that?'

'Nah,' said Mark III. 'I need a year off. I'm just going to chill out and relax.'

Alan looked baffled. 'But I programmed

you to want to destroy the world.'

'Sorry,' said Mark III. He popped a loaf of bread in his mouth and loped back inside the house.

Alan sighed.

Kevin Phillips gave Alan a look as if to say, 'I told you so.' Or it could have been a look as if to say, 'I need another biscuit.' It was hard to tell.

'He'll be back,' said Alan uncertainly.

Just then Mark III put his head round the door.

'See!' said Alan, beaming with joy.

'Can I borrow some money?' asked Mark III.

'Yeah,' said Alan, his shoulders drooping.

He handed Mark III some notes from his wallet, then changed his mind and handed him the whole wallet.

'Be careful,' said Alan. 'Phone me!' he called as the robot ambled up the path carrying a small rucksack.

'OK, let's forget about invading China or Russia or anywhere else,' said Alan, turning to Kevin Phillips. 'Let's just fly to London and destroy the world like I planned. I'll go and pack.'

Wilf felt the icy hand of fear grip his underpants. His stomach did a double backflip and his knees **badoinged** all over the shop. He needed to do something. He needed to stop Alan. But how?

He had to destroy the **most magnificent most marvellous most magical mechanical flying machine**. But the fence round it was locked and Alan had said there would be lions guarding it. And Wilf had a silly fear of being mauled to death by lions. Well, not that silly, come to think of it.

Wilf drew a picture of a lion.

Then Wilf tried to think of what could be worse than coming face to face with a lion. Wilf was scared of balloons and really, really scared of dentists.

Coming face to face with a lion who was also a dentist and holding a balloon?

Wilf needed a plan. He had a great **big old worry**. Then he had a great big old think. And he thought and thought until his brain needed a lie-down. And then he had an idea.

If he took a drawing pin, he could pop the balloon.

And if he wore his granny's false teeth, the lion dentist wouldn't be able to hurt his teeth.

But what could he do about the lion's appetite for small boys?

He chewed thoughtfully on his bubblegum and blew a bubble.

It popped.

That was it!

If he wadded up all the bubblegum he could find and threw it in the lion's mouth, the lion wouldn't be able to eat him.

Wilf drew this.

Wilf packed his rucksack with a drawing pin and a huge ball of bubblegum and he popped his granny's false teeth in his mouth.

Then he looked at the leaflet again.

NUMBER EIGHT said:

8) *Go to your happy place. Instead of thinking about what you are scared of, think about being somewhere nice, like a beach.*

133

Wilf imagined he was on a beach. He hoped he wouldn't get prickly heat from the sun. And he hoped he wouldn't see a crab. He *hated* crabs – they were all scuttly and crabby and they might nip his toes and then he might fall over and get seaweed on his face and *arrgggh*! The idea of sitting on a beach was making him feel worse.

He looked at **NUMBER NINE** on the leaflet.

9) *Try breathing deeply.*

Wilf started breathing deeply. He breathed as deeply as he could but then he started worrying that he might breathe in a gnat and then the gnat might lay eggs and then every

time he breathed out he would breathe out a

KERBILLION

baby gnats and people would call him 'gnat-breath'.

Wilf jumped up. He'd rather be fighting dentist lions than breathing in gnats and being nipped by crabs! He put Dot on his shoulders and rushed round to Alan's garden.

When he got there, he was delighted to see there were no dentist lions holding balloons. But there was the top of the **most magnificent most marvellous most magical mechanical flying machine** poking out from behind its sheet. Underneath was a huge launch pad and next to it a tall towering tower with lots of buttons that he

135

didn't want Dot to press. So he stuck the big ball of bubblegum to the fence and he stuck Dot to the bubblegum – for safekeeping.

Then Wilf tiptoed towards the control panel.

'What are you doing?' demanded Alan.

Wilf jumped and did a high sort of whinny of a scream.

'Nothing!' he said.

Although, because he was wearing his granny's teeth, it came out as 'Mmmmmfoooffffffimmmmmm!'

'What?' said Alan.

Wilf removed the teeth. 'Just looking at this stick,' he said, picking up a stick he'd spotted on the ground.

'Guards!' shouted Alan.

Wilf froze and looked round. Nothing happened.

'GUARDS!' said Alan, a little louder.

A small man eating a sandwich stepped out of a small beige hut next to the launch pad. He had a parting too far over to one side of his head. If you imagine a person's head is a clock, then a parting should really be somewhere between eleven and one o'clock. But this man's parting was at three o'clock.

The man-with-the-parting-at-three-o'clock swallowed his mouthful of sandwich, cleared his throat and said, 'It's actually "guard". Not "guard*s*". There's just me.'

'Where are all the others?' asked Alan.

'Pete's got a doctor's appointment and the others are on a training day, learning how to use the new Trespasser Destroying Equipment.'

'Where are the lions?' asked Alan.

'They got delivered to the wrong address,' said the man-with-the-parting-at-three-o'clock.

'Well, could you wrestle this boy to the ground?' asked Alan impatiently. 'He's trespassing and he's playing with a stick that belongs to Kevin Phillips.'

'There's nothing I'd like more than to wrestle that boy to the ground, but it's my knee, you see. There was an episode. Last week. It popped out. I wouldn't want a repeat of the episode,' said the man-with-the-parting-at-three-o'clock.

'Fine,' said Alan. 'Then could you liquify him please? With the new Trespasser Destroying Equipment.'

'I can't. I'm not on the training day. The others will be able to when they get back. You need a certificate,' explained the m-w-t-p-a-t-o-c.

'Well, just blast him to smithereens then!' said Alan tetchily.

The m-w-t-p-a-t-o-c produced some documents. 'The latest health and safety regulations say we should not attempt to blast objects as small as that small boy to smithereens. He's barely more than a smithereen as it is.'

Alan put his hands on his hips. 'Would it be too much to ask,' he said a little snippily, 'to just make him feel in some way scared and uncomfortable?'

'Of course not,' said the m-w-t-p-a-t-o-c.

'Thank you,' sighed Alan.

The m-w-t-p-a-t-o-c approached Wilf.

'Global warming is getting worse and it's partly your fault.'

'Oh. Sorry,' said Wilf.

'Will that be all?' asked the m-w-t-p-a-t-o-c. 'Because, strictly speaking, it's my lunch break.' As he spoke, he tried to flatten down his hair that was parted in the wrong place but it kept flipping back. 'Also, it's my birthday,' he added, producing a balloon from his hut.

'Aaaaah!' shrieked Wilf and popped the

balloon with his drawing pin.

The m-w-t-p-a-t-o-c looked at what used to be his balloon in surprise.

'Sorry,' said Wilf. 'I was worried it might pop so . . . I popped it.'

Alan and the m-w-t-p-a-t-o-c looked at Wilf.

'Well, anyway,' said Wilf, 'must get on. This stick isn't quite as interesting as I thought it was. Also, someone has slobbered on it – so I'll just go home. You don't need to liquify me or anything.'

'Good,' said Alan. 'Because I'm a little bit busy as a matter of fact. Doing secret things that are secret and that I couldn't possibly tell you about.'

As he spoke, a guinea pig tiptoed past in the background and made a break for freedom.

'Okey-dokey,' said Wilf, heading for the fence. 'But let's put it this way – *someone* is going to do *something* to *something big*. But that's all I'm saying.'

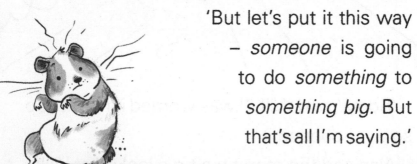

142

'Right-oh,' said Wilf, turning back again.

'And that *someone* is *someone you know.*'

'I see,' said Wilf. Because he did.

'But that's *all* I'm telling you,' continued Alan.

'Fair enough,' said Wilf, strolling off.

'Can you guess what it is?' asked Alan.

'No, I couldn't possibly . . .'

'Try!' insisted Alan.

'I have no idea . . .'

'Just guess!'

'Is the queen going to tickle an elephant?' asked Wilf.

'What?' said Alan.

'That's *someone I know* doing *something* to *something big.*'

'No, *of course* the queen isn't going to tickle an elephant. Why on earth would the queen tickle an elephant? Are you *trying* to annoy me?'

'No. It just seems to come naturally,' said Wilf honestly, peeling Dot off the fence with a squelchy *twang*.

'All right, all right, I'll tell you a bit more. 'The *someone* is *me* and the *something* is a *destroying* kind of thing. And the *something big* is the *world*. But that is all I'm telling you,' said Alan. 'Now, if you'll excuse me, I must go and power up my **most magnificent most marvellous most magical flying machine**.'

'You know, you don't have to destroy the world *today*. You could do it some other time,' said Wilf quickly.

'No, it has to be today,' said Alan. 'I've written it in my diary and everything.'

'But why do you want to destroy the world?' asked Wilf.

'Because . . .' said Alan, 'there are people who beep at you and people who push in front of you in queues and people who give you funny looks and insects that bite and germs that float and computers that won't work and there's mess and noise and crime and feeling scared and it has ALL got to stop.'

'Hmm. I don't know,' said Wilf thoughtfully. 'Some insects are really nice. I have a pet woodlouse called Stuart who's always kind and polite. I could introduce you—'

'No!' said Alan. 'It all has to stop! And I am going to be the one who stops it and then I will be world-famous and I will go down in history and everyone will know my name!'

'Yes, you mentioned that,' said Wilf. 'But

what about my idea of being famous for doing very good nice things? Or for doing unusual things like sitting in a bath of jelly for a fortnight?'

But Alan wasn't listening. He marched towards his **most magnificent most marvellous most magical flying machine.**

He whistled for Kevin Phillips and then the two of them climbed the steps of the tower, stepped through the door, and sat down. With a flourish, Alan pressed the

CLOSE button.

The door began to slowly, slowly – *vvvvvvvffffffffffffffffffff* – close.

Then Alan pressed another button which said

LAUNCH

and a loud rumbling *bbbbbbbbbbbbrrrrrrrrrrrr* could be heard.

Wilf realized what was happening and ran

quickly quickly up the steps of the tower, *tip tap tip tap tip tap*, and then hurtled – **thud thud thud thud** – towards the closing electronic door.

Vvvvvvvvvvvvvvffffffffffffff.

THUD THUD.

Vvvvvvvvvvvvvvvffffffffffffff.

Thud thud thud.

He was nearly there.

It was nearly closed.

He was nearly there.

It was nearly closed.

Vvvvvvvvvvvvvvvvffffffffff.

THUD THUD.

DOINK.

Wilf was too late. The door closed. And he bounced off the side.

OUCH.

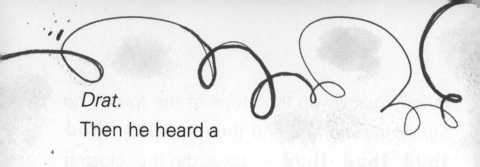

Drat.

Then he heard a

ZZZZZZZZZZSSSSSSSSSSSS SSSSSSSSSSSSSSHHHHHHHH

sound, and smoke poured out of the bottom of the **most magnificent most marvellous most magical mechanical flying machine**.

With Dot under one arm Wilf rushed down the steps, *scrambly slip scrambly slip scramble scramble scrape slip scramble scuff graze slip scramble*, until he got to safety.

They crouched behind the small wooden hut and watched Alan rising into the air on his **most magnificent most marvellous most magical mechanical flying machine**.

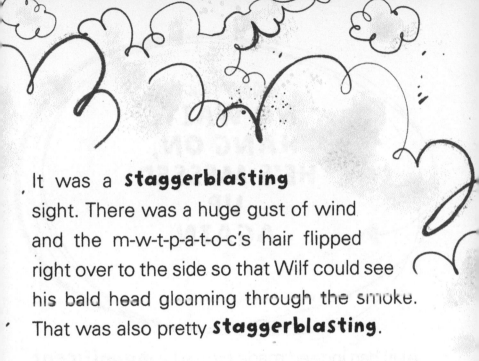

It was a **staggerblasting** sight. There was a huge gust of wind and the m-w-t-p-a-t-o-c's hair flipped right over to the side so that Wilf could see his bald head gloaming through the smoke. That was also pretty **staggerblasting**.

CHAPTER 8
NO WAIT, HANG ON, HE'S MESSED UP AGAIN

Alan had indeed made himself a **magnificent flying machine**. He had built a model of that most majestic of flying creatures – the daddy-long-legs.

Yes, a giant six-metre-high mechanical daddy-long-legs.

In the cockpit of his glorious craft, Alan pressed a button that said 'FORWARD'. The giant daddy-long-legs glided gracefully through the air. For a couple of metres. Then it shot off to the side. Then it went round and round a lamp post about twenty times, then it got sort of tangled up in a cloud, then one of its legs fell off, then another leg fell off – and then it went and sat on top of a tall building for about three days . . . . . . and everyone wondered if it was dead.

But no, it wasn't! Because on the fourth day it suddenly lurched off again (leaving a leg behind) and zigzagged and soared and dipped and plummeted and flapped around in

its own splendid straggly way, and at last Alan was on his way.

Next stop London.

Or maybe another cloud.

But then *definitely* London.

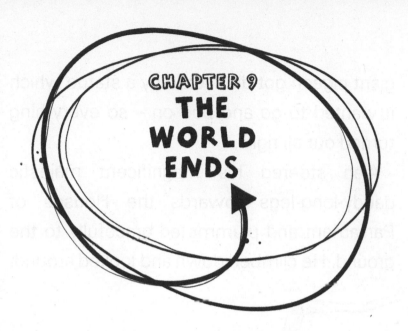

CHAPTER 9
THE WORLD ENDS

Three weeks later, the Houses of Parliament loomed into view. It had been a long, long, long and somewhat breezy journey. But, all in all, pretty uneventful for Alan. Except for when that other evil lunatic flew past on his giant mechanical pigeon which tried to eat Alan's giant mechanical daddy-long-legs. Luckily Alan and the daddy-long-legs got caught up in a cloud at just the right moment and the giant pigeon got distracted by a statue which it wanted to go and poo on – so everything turned out all right.

Alan steered his magnificent majestic daddy-long-legs towards the Houses of Parliament and plummeted gracefully to the ground. He climbed down and looked around.

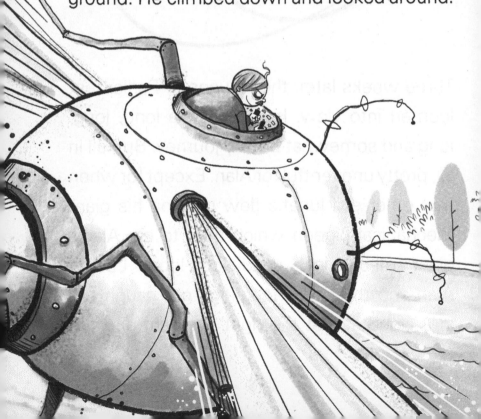

'London at last!' he said. 'First I shall destroy the world! Then, and only then, I shall have an ice cream.'

Alan turned to get his Big Gun Thingy, but suddenly stopped in his tracks. Someone was standing in his way. It was Wilf.

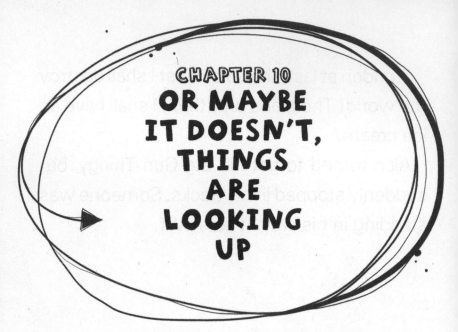

CHAPTER 10
OR MAYBE IT DOESN'T, THINGS ARE LOOKING UP

'How on earth did you get here?' Alan asked Wilf.

'I came by coach,' said Wilf.

Alan went a bit quiet and looked like he was having a thought that he wished he'd had some time before.

'Yeah, Dot and Stuart and I came a couple of weeks ago. We've been to all the museums *and* the Tower of London *twice*,' said Wilf.

Which, let's face it, was a little insensitive.

'Well, that's all very well, but I'm here now,' said Alan, 'and I'm going to kill you all. Yes. Until you're all dead. Deadity deadity dead. Deadity deadity dead dead dead. And what are you going to say then?'

'Not much,' said Wilf.

'NO. INDEEDY DOODY. INDEEDY DOODY DOO.'

Alan was in a very good mood at the thought of doing all this evil. You could tell because he was making up words and adding bits to words that already existed.

'YESSITY YESSITY YES YES YES.

Put that in your **PIPPITY POPPITY PIPES** and give it a great big large big smoke, **LOSERS OF LOSERVILLE!**'

Alan really didn't know when to stop talking.

'Oh I'm the baddest, I'm the baddest, I'm the

BIDDLY BODDLY BADDEST

in the whole wide worlderoony. And that is a fact-eration-istic-ism-onishment. Ation. Erality. Ington. Ism.'

Alan had finally stopped talking.

'ADOODLE DOO.'

Oh no, he hadn't.

Fortunately for everyone he was interrupted by another leg falling off the daddy-long-legs.

'Right, better get on with it,' said Alan. 'Where's my Big Gun Thingy?'

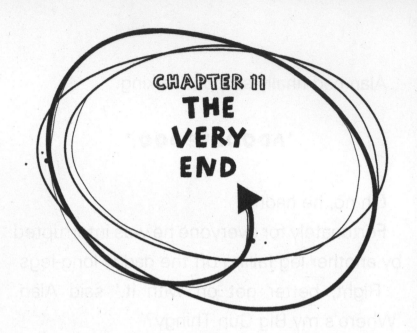

CHAPTER 11
THE VERY END

As Alan rummaged around in the daddy-long-legs' bottom, looking for his Big Gun Thingy, some people wondered how they could stop him destroying the world.

Some other people wondered whether they had turned their taps off or what they should have for supper – but they weren't really paying attention.

Most people felt quite worried and hoped

someone would do *something* before it was too late.

But who would that person be? There were a lot of people to choose from. For gathered in London at that very time were some of the world's most expensive suits. And inside some of those suits were some very clever and important people. And inside other suits were people who didn't have a clue but were hoping nobody would notice.

They had all been practising shaking hands and now they were all looking forward to lunch and hoping it wasn't spaghetti because that can be quite tricky to eat.

Meanwhile, Alan had found his Big Gun Thingy and also his walking boots which he'd been looking for everywhere.

'Right,' said Alan. 'Nobody move!'

Everyone stood very still except for Kevin Phillips who scooted along the ground on his bottom and barked happily.

'I am now going to destroy the world!' said Alan importantly.

All the people gasped. Well, most of them gasped. One of them gave a sort of wheezy cough and another one mouthed, 'What did he say?' to his wife, and a third one had just swallowed a boiled sweet the wrong way.

'Yes, oh yes,' continued Alan in his evil way. 'It's curtains for the world. And not nice flowery curtains. BIG curtains saying "THE END" on them.'

The people gasped again. And the wheezer wheezed a bit more. And the one with the boiled sweet thumped his chest.

'So does anyone have anything to say before I destroy the world?' asked Alan.

Everyone thought. Everyone with a beard scratched their beard. A couple of people thought they might have something to say but they didn't like being put on the spot.

Twelve more felt it was on the tip of their tongue. Someone near the back would have said something but he had a sore throat. The rest of them were too shy to speak in public.

'There's a phone call for you,' said a man with tiny ears.

Everyone tutted and sighed – if they'd known someone was going to come up with something *that* silly they'd have said something themselves.

'No. Really. There is.'

The phone was passed to Alan.

'Hello?' said Alan. 'I'm a little bit busy – can you call later?' Then suddenly his whole face lit up. 'LRX2FL309version8.4markIII!' he said. 'How are you? Where are you? I've been *so worried.*'

Alan listened. Kevin Phillips tilted his head to

one side. Everyone else waited and shuffled about while Alan said,

'UH HUH.
MMMM.
NO! REALLY?
HOW?
I SEE.
YES.
HMMMM.
RIIIIIIIIGHT.
OK. YES.
Just let me get a pen and paper.'

It turned out that someone had stolen Mark III's passport. And his iPod. And his wallet. And his phone. Or possibly he'd left them all on the train. He wasn't too sure.

While Alan was writing down the address of the nearest bank to Mark III so he could send some money to him, Wilf put Dot down and reached for his rucksack. He needed to check his leaflet. And draw a picture and come up with a plan. Because he was worried about big guns and loud noises and also dying. But just at that moment another leg fell off the daddy-long-legs right on to Wilf's rucksack.

Wilf was horrified. What was he going to do now? He didn't have his rucksack. He didn't have his leaflet. He didn't have a pen or paper. He didn't have a plan. He didn't have anything to help him. Most of all, he didn't have time to panic. And there was nothing he would have liked more than to have a big old panic. Or a great long hide under the duvet. But he couldn't.

IT WAS JUST WILF.
WILF AGAINST ALAN.

The future of the whole world depended on it. And that included Dot and Stuart. He *had* to do something. And he had to do that something

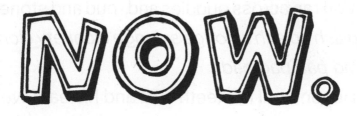

So Wilf grabbed the Big Gun Thingy and he

169

ran. He ran like an ant with its bottom on fire. He ran like a horse on skis. He ran like one of those lizardy things on holiday. He ran like he was running after the last ice-cream van in the world. He ran and he ran and he ran and he ran.

He looked round. Alan was chasing him!

Wilf ran across roads and parks and gravel. *Thud thud swish swish crunch crunch.*

In the distance, Dot followed, holding Pig. *Pad pad pad pad.*

Wilf ran across puddles and mud and stones. *Splash splash splodge splodge clonkety clonk. (Pad pad pad pad.)*

He ran until his teeth hurt and his ears were ringing and his heart ached. And all the while, Alan followed – getting closer and closer, closer and closer, closer and closer, closer and closer and closer until he was just there right behind him and suddenly:

WADOOMPH!

Alan grabbed Wilf and Wilf fell – and the Big Gun Thingy went *spinning spinning spinning spinning* . . .

And landed on Tower Bridge.

Alan leapt towards it but Wilf pulled him down.

Wilf leapt towards it but Alan pulled him down.

Wilf *crawled crawled crawled* but Alan *dragged dragged dragged* him back.

Wilf tried to break free, but Alan pinned him down.

Just then, Tower Bridge began to open slowly with a **CHUDDER CHUDDER AWWWWWW WWWW WWWWRK**.

Wilf and Alan wrestled and rolled and brawled and scrapped and tussled and scuffled and fought. And Dot crawled past, uphill now, *pad pad pad pad.*

Wilf and Alan thumped and kicked and bit and tugged and elbowed and cuffed and then just when it seemed that all was lost – Wilf wriggled! He slipped free and rushed up the hill of the opening bridge which was getting steeper by the second.

Alan hurled himself at Wilf and they rolled back down the hill.

While they were tussling and rolling – something else rolled. It was Stuart the woodlouse! He rolled out of Wilf's pocket, crawled on to Alan and bit him. (Yes, I know woodlouses/woodlice/woodlouseseseses don't bite, but that's because they've never needed to before.) Stuart needed to now and so he took a big chomp out of Alan's knee.

'Owwwwwwwwwww!' shrieked Alan. He grabbed his knee, letting go of Wilf. In an instant, Wilf leapt up to the top of the bridge and the Big Gun Thingy just in time to see Dot popping Pig down the end of it. It was ever such a nice fit. It just slid down and then wedged itself there.

Wilf grabbed the Big Gun Thingy but just then Alan grabbed his leg and held fast. He wasn't going to move. And that meant Wilf wasn't going to move.

Alan reached for the

 button, shouting. . .

'THE WORLD ENDS NOW!'

But Alan had forgotten that Wilf was blinking brilliant at hopping.

Wilf watched the other side of the bridge getting further and further away. He summoned all his strength and he did the *biggest* and *best* hop he'd ever done in his life.

As he did so, Alan slid down Wilf's leg and fell *down down down* into the River Thames below with a large *PLOP* (taking Wilf's shoe with him).

Wilf landed on the other side of the bridge. He aimed the Big Gun Thingy away from earth and into the sky and pressed the

 button.

Pig went falooping up into the sky at a

KERBILLION

miles an hour.

When it landed again (several days later) it was a bit more grey and a bit more shiny and it had one less ear.

A wisp of smoke emerged from the end of the gun.

I don't know if a gun can cough, but the gun coughed. And then it sort of gulped and creaked and cracked and went *sproing*. And then the words

'MALFUNCTION'

and

'FOREIGN OBJECT'

and

'URGH, PIG'S EAR'

and

'I'M BROKEN AND IT'S NO GOOD TRYING TO FIX ME'

flashed up on the screen.

Wilf threw the gun on the ground and jumped up and down on it for good measure. Dot snapped the trigger off, chewed it and threw it over her shoulder.

'Hooray!' shouted every single person in the world (except one).

'Boo!' (*splash*) shouted one person. (Can you guess who?)

Then the whole world jumped up and down and hugged each other and did skippety dances. Except for one person who stomped soggily towards his giant daddy-long-legs, got in it,

pressed

and went lurching off, zigzagging and soaring and dipping and plummeting and flapping sadly home (not before getting tangled up in a cloud for a few days).

And the whole world had a giant picnic and

then went home to watch the queen tickling an elephant on TV. She'd never done it before but she just fancied it.

Wilf and Dot and Stuart made their way home, tired and grubby but happy.

To celebrate, they had a peanut-butter sandwich and then they all shared some juice from Wilf's special cup that said 'Wilf' on it . . .

Because, suddenly, Wilf didn't feel so worried any more.

→ THE END!
(OF THE STORY,
NOT THE WORLD)

1. Alan is now a life coach.
2. Mark III teaches English as a Foreign Language.
3. Wilf's mum has a new (bigger) bin.
4. The killer sharks are now reformed and are just sharks. They have moved from the shark tank to an ocean.
5. The man whose sweet went down the wrong way has made a full recovery.
6. Kevin Phillips has a new squeaky toy.
7. Pig has a new ear.
8. Stuart has a tiny medal.
9. Wilf is still living in the same house and still goes to your school.

WHAT HAPPENS NEXT . . .

Does Alan give up
his evil ways?

Does Wilf need to save
the world again?

FIND OUT IN

OUT NOW!

wilfthemightyworrier.com
@quercuskids

GEORGIA PRITCHETT is the author of this book! Unlike Wilf, she's not afraid of anything. Oh, except maybe...

Sleepy flies

Hairy jumpers

Daddy-long-legs

Being more than ten minutes away from a snack...

For updates and news on Wilf and Georgia's worries (they have loads more!) visit wilfthemightyworrier.com